Second U.S. paperback edition 1997

The Library of Congress has cataloged the hardcover edition as follows:

Oxenbury, Helen.
Tom and Pippo and the bicycle / Helen Oxenbury. —
1st U.S. ed.
Summary: Because his toy monkey keeps falling off the back
of his bike, Tom envies Stephanie for having a big new bike with
a passenger seat at the back.
ISBN 1-56402-321-4 (hardcover)
[1. Bicycles and bicycling — Fiction. 2 Toys — Fiction.] I. Title.
PZ7.0975Tk   1993
[E] — dc20   92-42379

ISBN 0-7636-0162-4 (paperback)

2 4 6 8 10 9 7 5 3 1

Printed in Hong Kong

This book was typeset in Goudy.
The pictures were done in watercolor and pencil line.

Candlewick Press
2067 Massachusetts Avenue
Cambridge, Massachusetts 02140

TOM and PIPPO and the Bicycle

Helen Oxenbury

CANDLEWICK PRESS
CAMBRIDGE, MASSACHUSETTS

I like to ride my bicycle
in the yard.

Pippo always wants
to ride with me,
so I put him
on the back.

But when we go over
a bump, he falls off.

While I was making Pippo
feel better, Stephanie came.
She has a beautiful new bike.

I really need a big bike
with a real seat on the
back for Pippo, so he
won't fall off.

Stephanie's bike is
much better than mine.

Stephanie had a really good idea. She made a bed for Pippo in the wheelbarrow and tied it to the back of my bike.

Stephanie says she's sure
I'll get a big bike like hers
someday.

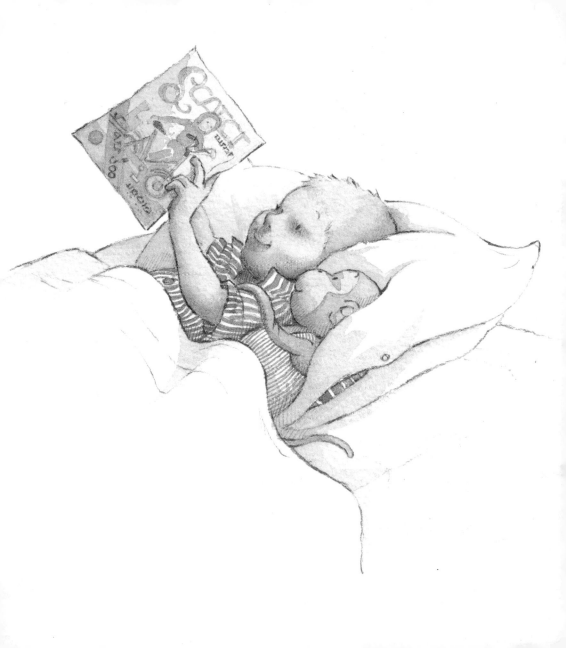